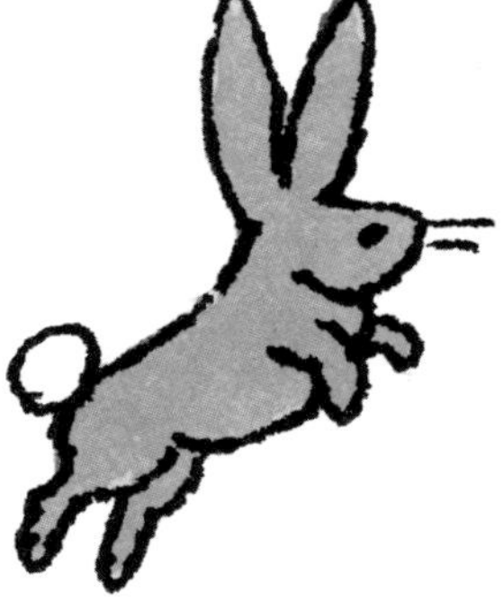

TEN LITTLE RABBITS

Ten Little Rabbits

By Maurice Sendak

HARPER
An Imprint of HarperCollinsPublishers

2

3

4

5

6

7

8

9

10

SO THEN—
HE MADE THEM VANISH AGAIN!

9

8

7

6

5

4

3

2

1

NONE

ALL DONE.

Ten Little Rabbits
Copyright © 1970 by Maurice Sendak
All rights reserved. Printed in the United States of America.
No part of this book may be used or reproduced in any manner whatsoever
without written permission except in the case of brief quotations embodied in
critical articles and reviews. For information address HarperCollins Children's Books,
a division of HarperCollins Publishers, 195 Broadway, New York, NY 10007.
www.harpercollinschildrens.com

Library of Congress catalog card number: 2023941550
ISBN 978-0-06-264467-1

Original Art Digitally Photographed by Elvira Piedra & Stephen Stinehour
Typography by Rachel Zegar
23 24 25 26 27 PC 10 9 8 7 6 5 4 3 2 1

Originally published in a different format by
The Philip H. & A. S. W. Rosenbach Foundation in 1970
First Picture Book Edition, 2024